Charlie And Isabella

Meet Jacob

Felicity McCullough

Series:
Charlie And Isabella's Magical Adventures

My Lap Shop Publishers
Plymouth, England
www.mylapshop.com

First Edition January 2012
Published by:
My Lap Shop Publishers
91 Mayflower Street, Unit 222
Plymouth, Devon PL1 1SB
United Kingdom
Tel: +44 (0)871 560 5297

www.mylapshop.com
www.goatlapshop.com

Joyeeta Neogi produced these delightful illustrations. The author is very grateful that she took great care to illustrate the story as accurately as possible.

The publisher thanks David Brown for his support and help in bringing these series of books to publication.

ISBN - 978-1-78165-005-9

Dedication

To My Ever Loving Father

Felicity McCullough

Charlie and Isabella had enjoyed meeting Sophie and were back at home in the Golden Berry Glen.

It was a new day and the sun was shining.

Isabella said to Charlie that she wanted to get to know some more humans, as Sophie had been the first that the two Angora goats had met. They had helped Sophie get safely home, after she had become lost in the woods.

The two golden haired Angora goats, decided to go to the creek at the end of the forest. They set off for a long journey, and packed some golden berries to take with them.

It was late in the afternoon, when they arrived at the creek.

By the water, was a boy throwing stones. He had been watching the ripples that they made, after each stone plonked into the water.

Charlie said that he was curious about this boy. He said to Isabella, "Let's go and talk to him". Isabella agreed. They stood behind the boy and waited for the boy to spot them.

The boy looked around to pick up another stone, and was startled to see two golden goats.

The boy exclaimed! "My, you are two gorgeous goats, with your shining coats of gold." He was shocked, when Isabella asked him what he was called.

"You talk! I'm Jacob." The boy yelled with delight.

The two goats introduced themselves.

Charlie asked Jacob whether he knew Sophie. He said that he didn't.

Charlie asked Jacob what he had been doing.

Jacob said that he had nobody to play with, and was bored.

Isabella suggested that they take Jacob for a ride in their cart.

Jacob jumped with joy, and said he would love to go for a ride.

Both goats knew that they could fly, and smiled at each other. They thought that they would surprise Jacob and secretly agreed after about five minutes, that they would take off.

"You fly! Screamed Jacob.

"Yes." Isabella said, turning her head.

Charlie said to Isabella lets go really fast.

Isabella agreed reluctantly.

Soon they were speeding over the tops of the trees.

Suddenly, BANG!

They had hit something.

Isabella had been hit by a telephone wire in the face.

The cart dived towards the ground.

It took all of Charlie's strength to hold Isabella and steer the cart.

Charlie landed the cart, with a great thud.

Charlie asked Jacob whether he was alright.

Jacob picked himself up off the ground from where he had fallen out of the cart.

"Yes." He said. "I'm fine."

Charlie called to Isabella, who was lying lifeless on the ground. He started whining an awful sound.

Jacob sprung into action. He could see a farm house nearby, and ran for help.

Charlie held Isabella in his forelegs. He tried to give her the kiss of life.

Jacob returned, after having fetched the farmer.

The farmer immediately took over from Charlie, and attended to Isabella. Isabella opened her eyes.

The farmer told her to rest. He picked her up and carried her to his goat pen.

He placed her on a deep bale of hay. The farmer said that he would go and fetch some fresh herbs.

Charlie asked Isabella, how she was.

Isabella said that she had a very bad headache, and a lump on her forehead, where she got hit.

Jacob said that he was sorry that Isabella had been hurt.

Isabella asked where she was, as she was still somewhat dazed.

Jacob explained that this was farmer Giles' goat farm. He pointed out to Charlie and Isabella, the other goats in the next goat pen.

Charlie started talking with the other goats, whilst Jacob looked after Isabella.

Charlie returned and told Isabella that the farmer treated the other goats very well, and provided all their food. They said it's just like a hotel, he told Isabella.

Charlie and Isabella decided to stay, at least until Isabella had fully recovered.

The farmer returned. He made a big fuss over Isabella, and hand fed her. The farmer also gave Isabella some water.

The farmer told Jacob that the goats would have to stay there, for the time being, and that Jacob could visit them anytime he wanted to.

The farmer returned to the farm house.

Jacob said that he had a wonderful time, and that it had been great fun. He promised to return again tomorrow, to check if everything was alright with Isabella.

Charlie and Isabella said that they had very much enjoyed meeting Jacob. They said when they had been flying very fast, that it had been the best time of their lives.

Jacob waved goodbye.

Charlie and Isabella waved goodbye to Jacob, as he walked away down the lane.

After Jacob had left, Charlie and Isabella began talking with the other goats and told of their adventures.

Books In The Series:

Charlie And Isabella's Magical Adventures

Charlie And Isabella's Magical Adventure

Charlie And Isabella Meet Jacob

Charlie And Isabella's Second Adventure With Jacob

These books may be obtained from the publisher:

My Lap Shop Publishers
91 Mayflower Street, Unit 222
Plymouth
Devon UK
PL1 1SB

www.mylapshop.com
www.goatlapshop.com
Tel: 44 + (0)871 560 5297